ULTIMATE MILITARY MACHINES

WARSHIPS

Tim Cooke

A+

Smart Apple Media

This edition published in 2013 by
Smart Apple Media, an imprint of Black Rabbit Books
PO Box 3263, Mankato, MN 56002

www.blackrabbitbooks.com

Brown Bear Books Ltd.
Editorial Director: Lindsey Lowe
Managing Editor: Tim Cooke
Children's Publisher: Anne O'Daly
Picture Manager: Sophie Mortimer
Creative Director: Jeni Child

Library of Congress Cataloging-in-Publication Data
Warships / edited by Tim Cooke.
       p. cm. -- (Ultimate military machines)
 Includes index.
 Summary: "Describes warships as used in the military, including specs, weapons, and crews. Includes the types of
missions they are used in and diagrams of the interior of the vehicle. Features a gallery of warships from around the
world."—Provided by publisher.
Audience: Grades 4-6.
 ISBN 978-1-59920-824-4 (library binding)
1. Warships--United States--Juvenile literature. I. Cooke, Tim, 1961-
V765.W3644 2013
 623.8250973--dc23
                              2012006751

Printed in the United States of America at Corporate Graphics,
North Mankato, Minnesota

Picture Credits

Front Cover: U.S. Navy

Brian Burnell: 29br; National Defence, Canada: 29tr; PLAN: 28; Robert Hunt Library: 05bl, 20, 21tr, 21b, 22/23, 22br, 23bl; U.S. Department of Defense: 04br, 05t, 15cr, 16; U.S. Navy: 04bl, 06, 07tl, 07br, 08, 09tl, 09br, 10tr, 10bl, 11c, 11br, 13tl, 13cr, 13br, 14, 15tl, 15br, 17cr, 17bc, 18cl, 18br, 19, 24tl, 24br, 25, 26tl, 26br, 27; Windmill Books: 12.
All Artworks: Windmill Books.

Key: t = top, c = center, b = bottom, l = left, r = right.

PO1438
2-2012

9 8 7 6 5 4 3 2 1

CONTENTS

INTRODUCTION

From wooden Greek galleys to vast battleships bristling with huge guns, warships have provided vital defense for nations around the globe. Throughout history, warships have become faster, stronger—and ever more deadly.

LONG-RANGE

5-inch gun turret

▲ USS *John S. McCain* fires a long-range missile.

AGE OF IRON

The mid-19th century brought a huge change to warships. Steam engines replaced wind power and iron replaced wooden hulls, making ships faster and stronger.

CIVIL WAR SHIPS

The ironclads *Merrimack* (left) and *Monitor* clashed at Hampton Roads in 1862 in the first battle of iron warships.

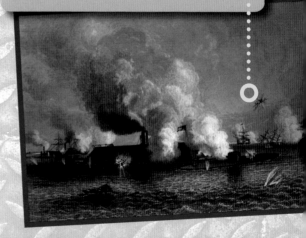

IRONCLAD: An armor-plated ship used in the Civil War (1861–1865).

USS NEW JERSEY

Four 12-inch guns for main armament

Early camouflage pattern

▲ In World War I (1914–1918), warships escorted convoys of merchant ships.

NAVAL WARS

World Wars I and II saw rapid developments as nations raced to build the most powerful fleet. Ships became heavier but faster. Guns became more powerful.

USS NEVADA

OCEAN BATTLES

In World War II (1939–1945), fleets clashed on oceans from the Pacific to the South Atlantic. By the end of the war, however, warships were becoming less important than aircraft carriers.

▲ USS *Nevada* bombards Iwo Jima in February 1945. US Marines landed and captured the Pacific island from the Japanese.

CONVOY: A group of ships traveling together for safety.

WHAT IS A WARSHIP?

A warship is an armed ship that fights other ships.
Modern naval warfare is based on aircraft carriers,
so the warship's job today is to protect a carrier.
That job can be done by destroyers, cruisers,
and frigates.

DESTROYERS

Destroyers are only medium-sized, but they move fast. Usually, their job is to protect other warships. They often carry guided missiles.

USS MILIUS

Landing deck for a Seahawk helicopter

Tomahawk cruise missile storage

GUIDED MISSILE: A missile that can be steered in flight.

USS SAN JACINTO

SPECIFICATIONS
Displacement: 9,600 tons (9,754 t)
Complement: 400
Length: 567 feet (173 m)
Max speed: 32.5 knots (60 km/h)

CRUISERS

Only the aircraft carrier is bigger than a cruiser. Cruisers can move very fast through the water. They carry a range of different weapons and are good multitaskers.

USS DOYLE

Sonar navigation equipment

Anti-aircraft gun

FRIGATES

Frigates are the smallest warships; they are less than half the size of a cruiser. A frigate often has only one task, such as escort duty or antisubmarine warfare. The US Navy is phasing out frigates in favor of more flexible cruisers and destroyers.

COMPLEMENT: The number of crew on a ship.

WARSHIP ROLE

In the early 20th century, battleships were huge. With the rise of air power in World War II, it became important to have fast vessels to protect carriers. Three classes of ships evolved to fill the role: cruisers, destroyers, and frigates.

● CRUISER ROLE

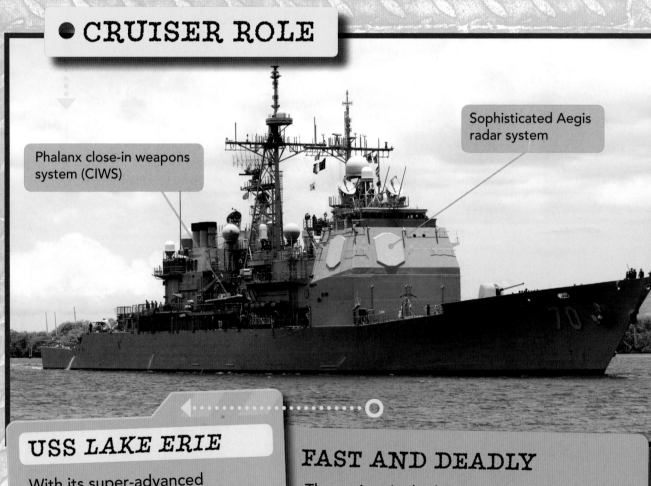

Phalanx close-in weapons system (CIWS)

Sophisticated Aegis radar system

USS LAKE ERIE

With its super-advanced computer systems, a cruiser can intercept and destroy missiles in midair before they get anywhere near their target.

FAST AND DEADLY

The cruiser is the biggest class of warship. Its job is to protect itself and smaller ships from air missiles and torpedoes. It carries high-tech sensors and weapons that can hit a target 500 miles (800 km) away.

CLASS: A group of ships that share the same basic design.

USS PORT ROYAL

◀ The Ticonderoga-class cruiser USS *Port Royal* was deployed in the Persian Gulf to support the War on Terror in 2011.

HUNTERS OF THE SEA

Cruisers can do many different jobs. With their powerful surveillance equipment, they are used to hunt enemy submarines in the sea or shoot down enemy aircraft high above using deadly cruise missiles.

READY FOR ACTION

Cruisers are known as "Battle Force Capable," meaning they have many combat roles. Other ships rely on them for backup in battle situations. They support carrier groups as well as amphibious task forces.

USS ANZIO

▶ The cruiser USS *Anzio*, on the left, sails with a supply vessel from the French navy (right) as it prepares to be resupplied at sea.

SURVEILLANCE: Secretly watching the enemy—often from a distance.

DESTROYERS AND FRIGATES

These warships may be smaller than carriers or cruisers, but they play key roles in an effective naval fleet.

SPEED KINGS

Destroyers are like mini versions of cruisers, but they are so fast they are called "greyhounds of the sea." Their speed, firepower, and surveillance capability make them great protectors of bigger ships.

● PROTECTOR

ESCORT DUTIES

Refueling at sea is vital to increase a ship's range so that it can avoid long trips to port. But the maneuver leaves a ship vulnerable while it is taking on fuel.

◀ A French destroyer (left) guards the carrier USS *Ranger* as it refuels from a supply tender.

RANGE: The distance a ship can sail before it has to refuel.

SMALL BUT STRONG

Frigates are small and relatively cheap, but they are built to last. They can take a lot of damage and still be seaworthy. They don't pack the same punch as a cruiser or destroyer, but they play a key role in destroying enemy aircraft, submarines, and warships.

USS THACH

USS *Thach*'s air-search radar

Guided-missile fire control system

TOUGH GUY

The USS *Samuel B. Roberts* sails alongside an aircraft carrier. The guided-missile frigate hit a naval mine in the Persian Gulf in 1988 during the Iran–Iraq war. The damage would have sunk most ships— but frigates are tough. The *Roberts* survived the blow and was repaired.

SUBMARINE: A vessel that operates out of sight under water.

WARSHIP FIREPOWER

Today's warships have all types of modern weaponry on board. Computerized missile technology is increasingly important. But the old-fashioned gun still has a role to play. Ships have carried guns for hundreds of years. Today, guns are used for close attack and defense.

BIG GUNS

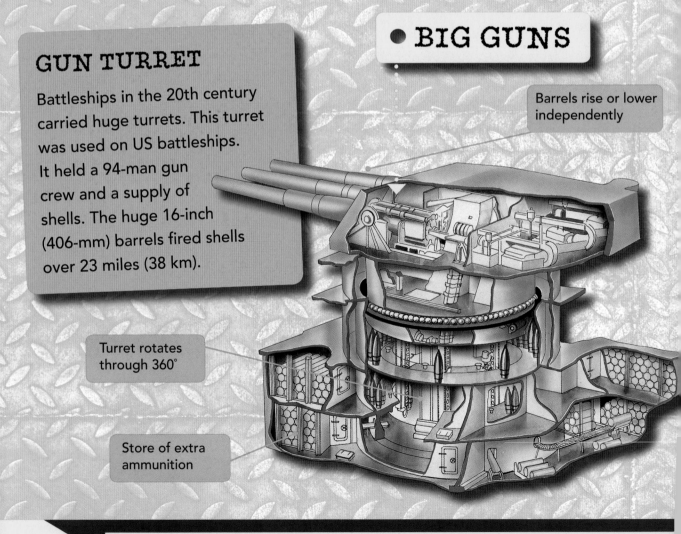

GUN TURRET

Battleships in the 20th century carried huge turrets. This turret was used on US battleships. It held a 94-man gun crew and a supply of shells. The huge 16-inch (406-mm) barrels fired shells over 23 miles (38 km).

Barrels rise or lower independently

Turret rotates through 360°

Store of extra ammunition

TURRET: A rotating tower that carries a gun on deck

TARGET PRACTICE

Sailors on the guided missile destroyer USS *Lassen* fire a machine gun at an inflatable target, nicknamed the killer tomato. Practice exercises at sea ensure that everyone knows his or her job if the ship does come under attack.

MK-75 GUN

The guided missile frigate USS *Thach* fires the Mk-75 76mm gun mounted on its front deck.

"The most challenging gunnery is firing from a moving platform at a moving target..."
NAVAL TRAINER

▶ A Phalanx close-in weapon system (CIWS) fires on USS *Juneau*. The CIWS shoots down antiship missiles.

CALIBER: The size of shell fired from a gun.

13

MISSILE POWER

Missiles are the biggest weapons on modern warships. Missiles can strike targets on water or on land, in the air, or even underwater. The first missiles were used by the Germans in World War II. The V-1 and V-2 flying bombs were guided by autopilots.

VERSATILE

An RGM-84 Harpoon anti-ship missile fires from USS *Gettysburg*. Harpoons can be fired at targets up to 150 miles (240 km) away in any kind of weather, so they are useful weapons.

Modern warships can hit targets hundreds of miles away and out of sight range using today's weapons.

● HARPOON

AUTOPILOT: A system that guides a missile without human assistance.

TOMAHAWK

LONG RANGE

A Tomahawk is launched from the cruiser USS *Shiloh* during Operation Iraqi Freedom in 2003. Tomahawks are carried on some classes of cruisers and destroyers.

NUCLEAR WARHEAD

Tomahawks have the longest range of any missile in the US Navy. The missile can be adapted to carry a nuclear weapon. It travels up to 550 miles per hour (880 km/h).

TORPEDO

A MK-46 Torpedo fires from a US Navy guided missile destroyer. It can be fired from ships, submarines, helicopters, or airplanes. Ships carry antisubmarine rockets (ASROCs) for more protection.

STANDARD

LIVE-FIRE TESTING

The navy's most popular medium-range antiaircraft missile is the Standard. It can shoot down airplanes up to 100 miles (160 km) away.

WARHEAD: The part of a missile that carries explosive material.

WARSHIP CREW

A warship needs a crew of trained personnel to function. Numbers are limited, so each sailor has his or her own special skill. A small frigate has a crew of about 300, while a larger cruiser might have about 800 crew and 50 officers.

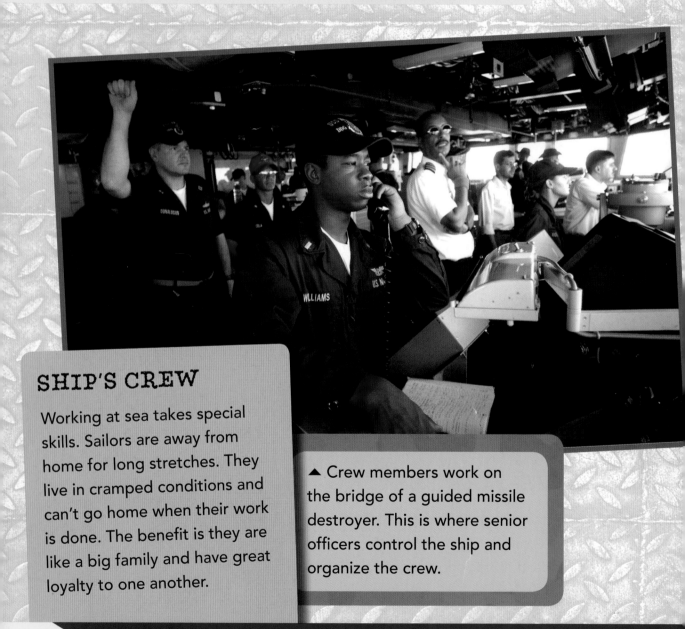

SHIP'S CREW

Working at sea takes special skills. Sailors are away from home for long stretches. They live in cramped conditions and can't go home when their work is done. The benefit is they are like a big family and have great loyalty to one another.

▲ Crew members work on the bridge of a guided missile destroyer. This is where senior officers control the ship and organize the crew.

OFFICERS: The senior personnel who command a ship.

COMPLEMENT

A ship's complement is made up of crews. Each crew does a different job. There are deck crews, weapons crews, engine crews, and communications crews. The sailors are supported by other personnel, including kitchen and medical staff.

FORMAL DAYS

Sailors "man the rails" on the aircraft carrier USS *George Washington*. On formal ceremonies, such as arriving in port, sailors have to wear full dress uniforms.

"Our Nation is diverse; our Navy must be no less so."
VICE ADMIRAL HARRY B. HARRIS, U.S. NAVY

EXPOSED

Some navy jobs can be very dangerous. In high winds or rough seas, all work on deck is potentially risky. Crew members are trained to keep an eye on each other as they work.

◀ Line handlers prepare ropes on the main deck of the USS *Blue Ridge* during a replenishment at sea.

REPLENISHMENT: A technical term for restocking a ship with supplies.

JOBS ON BOARD

Alongside its complement and officers, a ship also carries staff corps. These support staff do the same jobs as their equivalents on land. They work as scientists, engineers, doctors, nurses, cooks, and chaplains—but on a ship.

The US Navy is the largest in the world. Almost 330,000 personnel work for the navy with over 100,000 reserves.

SILENT SIGNALS

A signaler uses a semaphore to communicate with another ship. Semaphores are used because they can't be picked up by radio or other types of surveillance.

KEEPING WATCH

A sailor looks through binoculars on the frigate USS *Klakring*. Despite a ships' high-tech equipment, the human eye is still the best way to spot anything unusual in the sea.

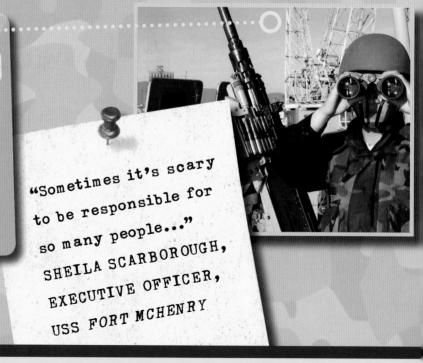

"Sometimes it's scary to be responsible for so many people..."
SHEILA SCARBOROUGH, EXECUTIVE OFFICER, USS FORT MCHENRY

SEMAPHORE: A messaging system that uses two flags to spell words.

SPECIAL FORCES

Modern warships often carry members of special forces. These elite fighters are trained for missions that require expert knowledge and skills, in or on the water, or on land. These forces began in World War II when warfare became more advanced.

ELITE FORCE

"The only easy day was yesterday."
MOTTO OF THE NAVY SEALS

◀ SEALs prepare to search a suspicious-looking vessel.

ALWAYS PREPARED

The US Navy elite force are the Navy SEALs. They are trained for special operations not only at sea but also in the air and on land. They can join any ship for a mission where they might be needed.

SEALS: Stands for sea/air/land special forces troops.

WARSHIP HISTORY

Sea battles have occurred for almost as long as people have gone to sea. The first warships were galleys with oars. Later, galleons had huge sails and rows of cannons. In the 20th century, warships helped decide the two world wars and were part of nearly every major conflict.

NAVAL RACE

Before World War I (1914–1918) Germany built a strong fleet. But after it was defeated by the British Royal Navy at Jutland, the German fleet retired to port. Jutland was the war's only major naval battle.

▼ The British Royal Navy and the German Imperial Fleet fought the Battle of Jutland in May 1916.

Smoke from coal-fired boilers

Sailing in line allows guns to fire broadsides on either side

BROADSIDE: Simultaneously firing all the guns on one side of a ship.

WORLD WAR II

Unlike World War I, World War II (1939–1945) was fought as much at sea as on land. Convoy routes across the Atlantic Ocean and Mediterranean Sea were fought over in the early part of the war. Later in the war, much of the military action involved the US fleets in the Pacific Ocean.

CONVOYS

It was crucial for the Allies to keep a supply route open across the Atlantic. As a defense against German U-boats (submarines), warships accompanied convoys of merchant ships.

D-DAY

On June 6, 1944, more than 5,000 warships and merchant ships took part in the D-Day landings on the French coast. They carried troops across the English Channel for the invasion.

▼ Allied landing craft carry troops from a warship to the beaches of Normandy on D-Day.

LANDING CRAFT: Flat-bottomed boats for landing troops on beaches.

PACIFIC WARFARE

When Japan bombed Pearl Harbor in Hawaii on December 7, 1941, the United States joined World War II. From then on, many of the naval and air battles that would prove decisive to the outcome of the war were fought in the Pacific Ocean.

EYEWITNESS

"A terrible explosion caused the ship to shake violently. I looked at the boat deck and everything seemed aflame."
CPL. E.C. NIGHTINGALE,
USS *ARIZONA*,
PEARL HARBOR

AMBUSHED

The attack on Pearl Harbor was meant to disable the US Pacific Fleet. The Japanese sank four battleships and damaged eight; all but two of the damaged ships were quickly repaired.

BOAT DECK: The level of a ship where the lifeboats are kept.

A NAVAL VICTORY

The Battle of Leyte Gulf in the Philippines was a key US victory. In October 1944, US bombers sank 26 Japanese ships there. The defeat marked the end of the Japanese navy.

KOREAN WAR

Much of the Korean War (1950–1953) was fought on land. US and Allied warships off the coast used their big guns to shell the Communist forces and cut their supply lines.

In Korea, US warships offshore bombarded enemy targets. Their role was like that of traditional artillery.

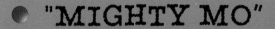

"MIGHTY MO"

SEA ATTACK

The USS *Missouri* fires its 16-inch (406-mm) guns near Inchon, Korea, in 1950. The *Missouri* was the last battleship built for the US Navy.

AROUND THE WORLD

For many years, different nations in the Middle East have been at war. American and international naval forces are deployed to the region's oceans in an effort to keep peace.

USS SHILOH

MISSILE LAUNCH

A no-fly zone was imposed on Iraq in 1991. When Iraq went to war against its Kurdish population in 1996, US ships fired Tomahawk cruise missiles against Iraqi air force targets.

TERROR RESPONSE

Following the terrorist attacks in the United States in September 2001, Operation Enduring Freedom was launched against terrorism. US warships were stationed in potential trouble spots across the globe to monitor any terrorist activity.

▶ A rigid hull inflatable boat (RHIB) leaves a frigate in the Gulf of Aden.

NO-FLY ZONE: An area where aircraft are forbidden to fly.

● USS BUNKER HILL

▼ USS *Bunker Hill* launches a Tomahawk missile on Iraq in 2003. More than 725 missiles were fired during the invasion of Iraq.

AFGHANISTAN

In 2001, US and Coalition forces invaded Afghanistan to fight the Taliban who supported the al-Qaeda terrorist organization. Afghanistan is landlocked, but warships supported the invasion with long-range cruise missile strikes.

STRIKE MISSIONS

Today the US Navy has a wide-ranging brief. It seeks to protect US interests by preventing the outbreak of faraway wars. It does this using its naval and air firepower to destroy selected targets with pinpoint accuracy.

LANDLOCKED: A country that has no coast and is surrounded by land.

GALLERY

Each class of warship has its own role. The class is usually named after the first ship that is built in it.

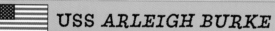
USS *COWPENS*

The USS *Cowpens* is a Ticonderoga-class guided missile cruiser. It has been in service since 1991.

SPECIFICATIONS
Displacement: 9,600 tons (9,754 t)
Complement: 400
Length: 567 feet (173 m)
Max speed: 32.5 knots (60 km/h)

USS *ARLEIGH BURKE*

SPECIFICATIONS
Displacement: 9,100 tons (9,246 t)
Complement: 323
Length: 509 feet (155 m)
Max speed: 30 knots (56 km/h)

The USS *Arleigh Burke* gives its name to a class of guided missile destroyer.

COMPLEMENT: A naval term for the full crew needed to run a ship.

USS *UNDERWOOD*

SPECIFICATIONS
Displacement: 4,100 tons
 (4,165 t)
Complement: 226
Length: 453 feet (138 m)
Max speed: 29 knots
 (54 km/h)

USS *Underwood* is an Oliver Hazard Perry-class guided missile frigate. It provided emergency help after the Haiti earthquake in 2010.

DISPLACEMENT: A ship's weight in terms of how much water it moves.

China's *Luyang II* is a guided missile destroyer. It has four antennae for complete radar coverage.

LUYANG II

SPECIFICATIONS
Displacement: 7,000 tons (7,112 t)
Complement: 280
Length: 505 feet (154 m)
Max speed: 30 knots (56 km/h)

ANTENNAE: A device for receiving or transmitting radio signals.

SPECIFICATIONS

Displacement: 4,695 tons
  (4,770 t)
Complement: 225
Length: 440 feet (134 m)
Max speed: 29 knots
  (54 km/h)

HMCS *OTTAWA*

Ottawa is a Canadian multi-role patrol frigate. It is designed to sail at high speed in rough seas and to deal with very cold weather.

HMS *DARING*

HMS *Daring* is an air defense destroyer first commissioned in 2009. Its radar can detect targets up to 250 miles (400 km) away.

SPECIFICATIONS

Displacement: 7,874 tons
  (8,000 t)
Complement: 190
Length: 499 feet (152 m)
Max speed: 29 knots
  (54 km/h)

RADAR: A system that uses radio waves to detect objects.

GLOSSARY

antennae (sing. antenna) Devices for receiving or transmitting radio signals.

autopilot A system that guides a missile without human assistance.

boat deck The level of a ship where the lifeboats are kept.

broadside Simultaneously firing all the guns on one side of a ship.

caliber The size of shell fired from a gun.

class A group of ships that share the same basic design. A class is usually named for the first ship built in it.

complement The number of crew on a ship.

convoy A group of ships traveling together for safety.

displacement A ship's weight in terms of how much water it moves.

galley A ancient type of ship that was propelled by oars; galleys were used as warships and also for trade.

guided missile A missile that can be steered in flight.

ironclad An armor-plated ship used in the Civil War.

landing craft Flat-bottomed boats for landing troops on beaches.

landlocked A country that has no coast and is surrounded by land.

no-fly zone An area where aircraft are forbidden to fly.

officers The senior personnel who command a ship.

radar A system that uses radio waves to detect objects.

range The distance a ship can sail before it has to refuel.

replenishment A technical term for restocking a ship with supplies.

SEALs Stands for sea/air/land special forces troops.

semaphore A messaging system that uses two flags to spell words.

submarine A vessel that operates under water, out of sight.

supply lines The means of getting provisions to troops in a war.

surveillance Secretly watching the enemy, often from a distance.

turret A rotating tower that carries a gun on deck.

warhead The part of a missile that carries explosive material.

FURTHER READING

BOOKS

Adams, Simon. *Warships* (War Machines). Smart Apple Media, 2009.

Alvarez, Carlos. *Ticonderoga Cruisers* (Torque Books. Military Machines). Bellwether Media, 2010.

Alvarez, Carlos. *Arleigh Burke Destroyers* (Torque Books. Military Machines). Bellwether Media, 2010.

Dougherty, Martin J. *Sea Warfare* Gareth Stevens Publishing, 2010.

Jackson, Robert, *Warships: Inside and Out* (Weapons of War). Rosen Publishing Group, 2012

Jackson, Robert. *101 Great Warships* (101 Greatest Weaopns of All Times). Rosen Publishing Group, 2010.

Rustad, Martha E. *U.S. Navy Destroyers* (Blazers. Military Vehicles). Capstone Press, 2006.

WEBSITES

www.pbs.org/wnet/warship/
PBS site on warship history to support the TV series *Warship*.

military.discovery.com/technology/ vehicles/ships/ships-intro/html
Military Channel videos of the Top Ten warships.

www.worldwarships.com
Fleet lists and photographs from the world's major navies.

militaryhistory.about.com/od/ shipprofiles/Ship_Profiles_Notable_ Warships.htm
Gateway page with links to pages about warship history.

INDEX